The ROYAL BABY

By Tony Bradman and Tony Ross

OXFORD
UNIVERSITY PRESS

THERE WAS ONCE A
beautiful princess
who married a
handsome prince.

It was the most wonderful wedding anyone could remember. But no sooner was it over than everyone started asking the same question.

'When will they have a baby?'

'Well, really,' said the Queen. 'That's none of their business!'

'Don't be angry,' said the Princess. 'They mean no harm.'

The Prince just blushed.

He blushed again a few months later
when the King made an announcement.

'Her Highness the Princess . . . is expecting a baby!' he roared.

The crowd cheered . . .

and then the questions really began.
'Ooh, a royal baby!' said somebody
in the crowd. 'Will it be a boy or a girl?'

'It's bound to be one or
the other . . .
or it might be both!'

The Prince and the Princess hadn't thought about twins . . .

'Will the baby be tall like the Prince's brother?'
said one of the palace servants.

'Or strong like his grandma, the old queen?'

'We hope not,' thought the Prince and Princess.

'Do you think the baby will be fair or dark?' said one of the maids.

'It might be hairy like the King's father, the old king.'

'Oh no, we don't want that,' thought the Prince and Princess.

'But will the baby be clever?'
said one of the King's counsellors.

'Of course it will
always have to
work very hard.'

'Maybe not all the time,'
thought the Prince and Princess.

'What do we want the baby to be?'
said one of the King's knights.

'SPORTY...
AND FEARLESS!'
roared all of the others.

'We'd just like our baby
to be safe,' thought the
Prince and Princess.

'What if the baby is musical,
like the Queen's sister?'
said one of the ladies-in-waiting.

Now that was an idea too awful to think about.

The questions went on as the Princess grew larger.
But the Prince and Princess knew they would
love their baby whatever it was like.

Soon everyone was
asking a new question.

When is the Princess
going to have that baby?'

Then one day the King made another announcement.

'The Royal Baby is . . . on its way!' he roared.

The crowd **cheered** and **cheered**...

and then went **very** quiet.

Everyone talked in hushed whispers and tippy-toed round the palace.

Everyone
waited
and listened
and kept
their fingers
crossed.

And everyone smiled
when they heard . . .
a baby's cry.

Of course, the baby was
beautiful and **special** . . .
as **all** babies are.

And now there was one last question.
'What will the baby **really** be like?'

We'll all
just have
to wait
and see.

For my three royal babies, Lily, Oscar, and Joe – T.B.

For Catherine and William – T.R.

OXFORD
UNIVERSITY PRESS

Great Clarendon Street, Oxford OX2 6DP

Oxford University Press is a department of the University of Oxford.
It furthers the University's objective of excellence in research, scholarship,
and education by publishing worldwide in

Oxford New York

Auckland Cape Town Dar es Salaam Hong Kong Karachi
Kuala Lumpur Madrid Melbourne Mexico City Nairobi
New Delhi Shanghai Taipei Toronto

With offices in
Argentina Austria Brazil Chile Czech Republic France Greece
Guatemala Hungary Italy Japan Poland Portugal Singapore
South Korea Switzerland Thailand Turkey Ukraine Vietnam

Text copyright © Tony Bradman 2013
Illustrations copyright © Tony Ross 2013
The moral rights of the author and artist have been asserted

Database right Oxford University Press (maker)

First published 2013

British Library Cataloguing in Publication Data available

ISBN: 978-0-19-273627-7

2 4 6 8 10 9 7 5 3 1

Printed in China

Paper used in the production of this book is a natural, recyclable product made
from wood grown in sustainable forests. The manufacturing process conforms
to the environmental regulations of the country of origin